Taylor,
i'm so +
for where u
i hope you enjoy!
the story mami.
call me so we can
talk about it !!

tAJA mAJA. D

TAJA MAYNIE
"bellhue"

Prelude
to King

Chicago
2017

Published by Taja Maynie
Chicago, USA
Printed by Blurb
San Francisco, USA

Grateful acknowledgment to Erykah Badu for melodies
and wisdom through song.
Lyrics from "Billies Blues" by Billie Holiday
Copyright 1936
All rights reserved
Lyrics from "Good Morning Heartache"
By Billie Holiday
Copyright 1946
All rights reserved
Lyrics from "Love Is Stronger than Pride"
by Sadé
Copyright 1988
All rights reserved

Cover designed by Taja Maynie
Cover Image designed by Casper Wright

For my mother
For you too

BOOK ONE

The word of my later years, for quite awhile, has been Melanin. It has encouraged in me, and many of my peers, a sense of entitlement to God. We have found, through our vitamin D sufficiency, that God is a Black Woman. That to find God, we must be introduced to travel as we come to know ourselves as having evolved the world. By this, we swear to never limit ourselves and our experiences, and to lend them to black men; to lift us up; to recount our divinity. How else does one begin to know thyself without meditating on the very energy that has birthed all of mankind? Exploration of the vastness of our world, introspection on the current state of the people, deliverance from our demons, and, then, rebirth. Being Black in the new age calls for all these things. It is the magic of melanin; the manifest destiny of colored people, and the revelation of God within us. It is the use and acceptance of creativity, the desire for more truths, and the realizations commonly found across the diaspora. The Western World, for all of its life, has hidden us from ourselves; has caused us to relinquish our God gift. We are demanding it back. After all, we have always been the vessel for humanity.

"My skin is light brown. My eyes are dark. So is my hair. I've lied about my name all my life; only some people know. I'm going to tell you what only some people know: My grandmother is white, but I prefer my African ancestry because, well, I never met her. It's actually difficult for a black girl in America to trace her African ancestry because she's living so dangerously free, and she shouldn't really remember the past all that much. They even want to take slavery out of the history text books. And my grandmother may be proud.

She probably never thinks of us- my mother, my brother and me. Sometimes I think of her, quite often actually, though, I never met her. She probably doesn't care to meet us. I'm glad my mother put up with me though. I'm ever grateful.

I'm writing this... I don't usually speak this way, but I write the way I like to hear things. Gutta.

Today is the second day of December. I would have called it the first to make it seem more dramatic, but I don't want to lie anymore.

I visited God this morning. I spoke to Her in the way I always do- like I trust Her with my secrets. Because most people can't keep secrets.

You see, even though I know you can't keep secrets, I've shared plenty with you in those few lines up there. Except this time, I want you to tell people about them, just in case they succeed in omitting slavery from the history text books.

My name was Nanita up until I was enrolled in pre-school as just Nani. I like being called Nanita sometimes. My black grandmother's side of the family still calls me Nanita because they named me. My white grandmother would probably like Nani better; or Dorothy or some corny shit. I named her Rue, even though we know her name is Theresa Dunigan. I'm no Dorothy. Nani means "beautiful," or sometimes "grace."

I think that is why I like to dance, if that makes sense. All I've ever wanted was someone to dance with. A man, preferably.

I had a man who was a real thinker. That is what made him a man. He's in Italy now, composing beautiful music for the world, probably to remind us that they would love to take slavery out of the history text books. They'll call it a clean slate, or, rather, equality. It's the end of 2017 and I still don't believe that shit exists. It's all fallacy. Our worlds are filled with fallacy. So how do you know if I am telling the truth? This is how you know: you feel."

*"**B**ack before I met my man, (I won't name him. That is the only thing I may keep a secret in case he returns one day.) I thought I had done enough to know everything about my 21 year old self. But you never really know unless you feel, and, baby, I had never felt until he touched me. He touched me so deep the imprint of his fingertips still lay on my skin. When I open my thighs, I smell him. He was real sweet, and swift too. He had all the things a woman so desires; like the will to live and not just exist. He vitalized me by Love. He made me feel Capital. LOVE. I had met him on the beach and see, I had been literally dreaming of him. One September I awoke with remembrance of a black beauty behind my eyelids. So eloquent in his stature, a vibrant melanin oozed from him. I felt the magnetic force from the dream change the course of my days. From that time, I knew something was imminent. He landed in my lap. I had his faith in my hands, but being so young I ruined something beautiful. Because people need so much. It was like I was a fist, and I clenched myself so hard out of fear and compression that I crushed him.*

He would talk to me about time and its relativity, mostly time's complacency. That's what I usually felt was complacency because we would dream of travel, but we worried about money. And since black people don't know anyone with money and there ain't no registration for the youth to take a free, 10-day trip to Africa like what is available for being a descendant of Judaism, we dreamed up ways we could attain some wealth. Dreams… That's where discontent begins."

CHAPTER 1

NANITA

I'm not writing anymore. In the midst of my catharsis, my good friend Blye knocks at my apartment door on 51st Street unexpectedly. I live alone. My brother stays on the west coast and my mother takes six day trips to Portland often. Blye showed up to my door with, instead of a chip, a parrot on his shoulder. He looked so gratis; so dangerously free. We hadn't spoken in months. Beautiful plumage the bird had though. Blye just stood there for a moment.

"Hey, you," I said. "What's to you?" and invited him in. He looked around my place wide eyed at my mess; I'm usually a pretty organized girl.

"I see you've been writing, Lil Luv, get a lot out?"

"Ah, I'm working on it. I ain't in too deep yet, you know it's a process."

"Sure I do... I just missed you, that's why I'm here."

I laughed. Blye was always popping in and out of my life, but I'm okay with casual.

He walked over to the windowsill where I had a laptop propped up and stuck his finger in the cup of half-empty tea I had sitting next to it.

"Your tea is cold. I'll make more. I figured you'd be up and at it by now so I didn't hesitate to come over," he said.

"I'm never expecting you," I quickly replied.

"That's what I like about us," Blye said with a half grin.

He walked toward me and we stood face to face without saying anything, just breathing and staring. I was never sure what he wanted from me. He walked around me and into the kitchen where he emptied the kettle and filled it with fresh water to boil. He turned the fire medium-high and gathered the ingredients for our tea: Honey, fresh lemon, ginger, two tea bags of Green and Mint tea- he knew what she liked.

"What's the story?" he yelled out to her from the kitchen.

I looked up from where I was sitting and staring out the window at the fallen leaves in the gutters, feeling outside of myself.

"Oh, it's about a girl. I'm not so sure yet. Just about a girl."

"Maybe she is like you?" he assumed. "If she is as whimsical and elusive, I may like her."

"Perhaps… I'm sure you'll like her. She is 'finding' herself, as they say; although we never do enough discovering."

"I would love to believe that we immediately know who we are, but I figure our intuition is, too, cultivated."

"It wouldn't be intuition then," I said, in response to his self-righteous remark.

"Perhaps it isn't. It is the discovery of the God within us."

This is always where our conversations ended up. Deep in the unknown.

"I figure it is too early to determine." It was only a quarter to eight.

I looked up at Blye who was now sitting on the counter top unbuttoning his jacket with a brightness in his eye that could have blinded me. We were quiet for awhile and I turned my back toward him, staring out at the gutters again.

I whispered, "you can't judge just now, just follow where I'm taking you." Blye knew that I was referring to the story I was developing and nodded. We heard the kettle sing.

Blye brought out two cups of what he must have thought the best tea he'd ever tasted. It was rich and thick like the spit swapped between lovers. I sipped it slow.

My taste buds went numb and when I could no longer taste the tea I felt compelled to talk until I thought my lips would follow suit. "What'd you have going on these past few days?" I asked. Blye laughed at how facetious I was being because we hadn't spoken in months. "I spent all of my time dreaming. It's funny, because I can hardly remember any of them except the most recent from this morning. You were in it. I thought to give you a call, but I knew you would enjoy my presence much more," he replied. "Charmed," I said in a British accent, although that is not my culture.

We sat. And we drank. And we sat some more. Suddenly he asked, "what do you get out of this?" I was bemused by the question. "Out of what?" I replied, not entirely sure I was ready for where the conversation was headed; probably deep into the unknown.

"This Life shit... What else am I ever talking about?" Blye said stiffly.

"Oh, I don't know," I replied.

"You're funny. You are always so modest in what you know. You always go 'oh well, I don't know' after you've said so much," Blye said, feeling like he was looking through me.

I admit she felt like glass. I said to Blye, "we never know shit for certain. Badu said 'the man that knows something knows he knows nothing at all.' And there is a *damn* thin line between fact and opinion." "You do know that everything 'fact' was once 'opinion'?" Blye said to counter my cynicism. "When we dropped a tab that one time, I was feeling some freaky shit. Like I was the all-knowing, or God was revealing Himself to me, telling me that I must trust what I believe. My truth is fact." I was listening to Blye and remembering how LSD made her feel: restless and filled, and very much outside of comfort. She, too, had felt God. She, too, had known truth. She, too, believed in significance. The world was in my face, and it felt like swallowing a quarter.

"But that feeling leaves," I said.

"That feeling doesn't leave. You let it go. You allow your worldly insecurities your truth. And they don't respect it. Your ego don't respect you."

I looked into Blye's eyes, smitten, and then to the left and right of his shoulders. There was no bird, but again a chip. I could see why we hadn't spoken in months. He was busy thinking; she was busy writing and figuring out how to decide between things. Blye would always put pressure on my decision-making, as if he was molding her, and she needed time to be indecisive, which is something he would not allow, so they cut their friendship for awhile but there were no hard feelings. We were funny that way.

Then, I began to feel glad that he popped up on me. I began to feel important and I told him that I would like to continue writing but that he could stay awhile and keep me company.

Blye left rather quickly, but I started by writing this:

"A woman is no greater than her man since like attracts like. And I figure that when a man can't get right, his woman ain't worth it. Either because of her own fragility, or his that she hasn't helped to mend. She may be worried about the sexism still prevalent in the 21st century and how there could, quite easily, be a highly respected woman beside every man, with the same status, in every field of study or labor. Because in the 21st century people make up stuff to fight about; People want something to fight for. I spent my life searching for a cause, and that is the root of my misery. I grew soporific in searching for my passion when I had a man and a pen that named me Surmount. But I don't trust myself- let alone trust those who hail me."

And that is where I ended.

It was after I had taken a year off from school that I began to notice this. After high school I just kept dreaming, which is how we drown. College became colloquial and I couldn't find the real point of it. But none of it could ever stop me. When my man left, I bossed up. I felt like I had to because we were originally gonna do it together, but, you know, everything *is* while it is... So I make my way, by God's grace, of course. Every sun up, I get it. I visited him in Venice last summer. I was enamored by the fullness in people's lives there. I couldn't ever imagine leaving. The Italian tongue was rich. Gold was in that water. It felt like we'd finally reached the land we spoke in our sleep about. And I didn't want to go. I almost never left. But he understands that I never want to be too comfortable again, so I dipped back to New York, the other city I fell in love with after moving from Chicago when shit got too stale. My city wasn't really made for my progression.

Anyway, that man always liked closeness and balance in things so it wasn't surprising that Venice, Italy felt so intimate. He was the only boy I dreamed about. I kept dreaming until he was a man and bigger than I knew him, but he always stayed down.

This was the way I began to *appreciate* security, but knew it wasn't something I had a real taste for and hoped that my buds may mature someday. I'm 26 now and very established in writing (it is the only other thing I have ever loved this way) and we, my man and me, have been sure to remain close.

CHAPTER 2

NANITA

"We cannot dismiss struggle. Struggle makes the story. Through all glory their is what seems, at the time, insurmountable struggle. Since I am writing, I am surviving. Since being in depression it is my only light.
I woke up one day paying too much attention to my misery. I left my joy at my feet; no longer wearing it atop my shoulders. My mother died on a trip home from Portland. What did I have to live for? I aborted a baby that was conceived out of boredom and anger for the only man that I love being so far across the seas. I have too much money and no vigor. I hate the man I love and I only dream in cycles. I am outside of myself."

I woke up looking out of my lofty window toward the city's skyline. The sun had just begun to peak. I could see its cantaloupe reflection on the building across from me. I don't know why, but I let out a sigh. I was beginning to believe I was mildly depressed because my expression usually came from a place of contempt. My purpose had gone missing, so I decided to take a trip to greet it again. I have some travel points available and my work schedule is as flexible as I like it. I mostly work from the road, and so, I booked a flight to Italy...

I needed to pack. I kept thinking to myself, "*lightly, darling... very lightly.*" In the middle of arranging my carry on, I decided to bathe instead since my flight wasn't out for another seven hours. I mixed a Eucalyptus and Spearmint aromatherapy bath foam in with the steaming, running water. Oh, the fragrance permeated. I lifted my sports bra above my head, I slid out of my panties and pranced around while the stone bathtub filled; turned on some soft Sade, but played it loudly. My stomach began to feel loose and bubble.

As I sat emptying myself and making room in my gut for spontaneity, I tried not to think about how I would be spending my time in Venice. (*Lightly, darling. Ever so lightly.*) That is where I left him, my man, along with my happiness. The tub was filled by the time I flushed so I turned off the water and washed my butt at the sink because I don't have a bidet. I went to the kitchen and measured out a cupful of Apple Cider Vinegar with the "Mother" ingredient in it and poured this into my bath water.

Sade was still playing and I bathed long while humming along. "*I won't pretend...*" I thought of people who may not have as much autonomy in their own life and thanked God.

After a cup of green tea with ginger and ginseng, I was ready enough for travel. I knew that I was going to need something to read while on the eleven hour flight, so I headed out to my favorite book store down the avenue.

I spent ten minutes outside of the store smoking a cigarette and watching the people, when just as I was about to go inside, a little boy ran into me and spilled his sherbet ice cream cone onto my tights. I imagined that a young mother would be running behind him to reprimand him for being so careless, but no one ever came. For the little boy had been alone in the city and was scurrying away from the parlor he had just taken the cone from without leaving a pence. The kid looked so busy and petrified that I may have slowed him down just enough to be caught. His eyes bulged as he didn't know what to say and he started to weep that all of his scurrying had been in vain. I had no idea of his endeavors and immediately thought to carry him along to buy another cone on me. "Come here, boy. Come here. We're sorry, now, aren't we, that we were in so much a rush. (*Lightly, darling... lightly.*)

I'll get you some more. Just slow down next time, ya know? Take your time with that delicious looking 'cream and maybe it'll last a bit longer, you see? Come along. We'll see to it that you get another. What'll you have? Double-scoop this time?" He smiled in the only boyish way he knew how and became elated that a stranger would offer him an ice cream cone after he had just stolen the one that was wasted. He dare not mention how he'd gotten it and opted to wait outside of the parlor while I replaced his cone, not forgetting the extra scoop. He preened himself as I handed him the sugar cone and he prattled the entire way back to the book store. I guess I had made it okay through my considerateness for him to tag along. But strangely I did not mind the kid's company. "Do you like to read?" I asked him. "Yeah, but I ain't got much books, Ma'am." I was taken aback by the way he addressed me and laughed at his partial politeness. "You're cute, kid. What they call you?" "I'm Black," and after a while, "That's my name," he said. I was quiet. I thought of what that color said. I thought of what people thought about his name *being* his color, and if people were more afraid of *him* or his name and color. I think pigment will always be a boulder since the paler you are, shit, the bolder.

We landed at the book store with my faith in this kid's hands. He had a lot of substance to be so young. It comes with the territory of having dark skin. I told him to follow me in and take a look around a place that could change his life. His eyes gleamed at the shelves and his nostrils filled with pages. I recognized a sense of peace through him and I knew that I, too, had the power to Create something. And, so, we began...

Black split from me once we entered the store and engulfed himself in the shelves of books. I grinned pensively and hopeful, and went on to the "Classic Novels" section. I had wanted a particular tone of book and decided on a Baldwin novel I had not yet read (if I could find one). Black seemed more drawn to classic literature in the sense of Shakespeare and romantic poets like Woodsworth. He was twelve, but very absorbent. I could tell he'd experienced some irresponsible, explicit content wherever he had come from, but I wouldn't dare bother him with it now.

I took my time with the shelves. Once I picked up a hardback book of Baldwin's, I knew it to be one I hadn't rummaged through since the latest publications were usually paper covers. I took to it and sat down to read while allowing Black to enjoy his indulgence in the building blocks of books. Was I the only one who could see his utter excitement?

I had gotten to the fifteenth page when Black plopped four books down on the wooden, vintage looking bench I was sitting on. There was an orange cover with a dark silhouette with *Little Bee* written on it that looked like something I would enjoy. There was *A Midsummer Night's Dream*; there was *The Rime of the Ancient Mariner*; there was *The Bluest Eye* by Toni Morrison. I was pleased. I asked, laughing, "What you know about Shakespeare, Young?" He said, "a lil' something." I told him I was ready if he was and we proceeded to the treasurer whom I would leave plenty pence with for the legal purchase of the five books Black and I had. This collection seemed fresh for him and that is what made me glad.

There was four hours left until my flight, so I called up my old man in Venice since that is where I left him. "Hello, Lady. What are you doing? I thought maybe I was dreaming when I saw you calling. I haven't heard from you in a few weeks. I know that you are all right. You are always all right. Do you still love me, Lady?"
I laughed before I could even get one word out. This is why I still love him. "Lady is the name of a dog," I said. Then, "I am coming to see you. I have a flight out in a few hours. I will arrive around high noon. Do you have time to see me?"

Black was still walking alongside me. The other end of the line was quiet for a moment. Suddenly he said, "I have a showcase in Morocco next week. This is perfect timing. You are so dazzling. You are the jazz that soothes me. Come now. I won't wait." Shit only went this smoothly when we didn't label ourselves. "I may bring someone along. I just met him; *un petit garçon*. I want to show him something." We hung up.

CHAPTER 3

BLAQUERAN

She never invited me home, but always welcomed me. I had never listened to so much of what a woman said, except *she* made me feel like the ears of Dumbo. Meeting her at The Last Book Store was like walking into Heaven.

She didn't know that it was, but on my thirteenth birthday Nani birthed me in a way. We went to Italy where I met an old friend who she referred to as "ours." The *Biennale d'Arte Contemporanea Muro Dipinto*, or Painted Wall Festival, was going on that year.

It was frightening there at first because we were the darkest things, but the natives were so full and inclusive. I had never experienced that back home *where they treat the Arabs and the Spanish and the Blacks wrong*. (There he go with that song.) Something about home was darker than my complexion and had a reluctance to let in light. Back in Dozza, you couldn't avoid anyone because they truly believed in closeness. This rarity helped me to cultivate myself… to reinvent and appreciate in value.

There is a lot of bright color on the brick in Italy, so people stood out that much more. When we arrived from Venice into Dozza, a man with fresh snow for teeth smiled at us. He looked at me then at Nani who was blushing, walked up to us and kissed her neck. Before taking her luggage, he introduced himself to me.

"Zig," he said with his right arm extended. I took his hand firmly. "Black, Sir. Nice to meet you. Na has told me much." Zig took Na's luggage and said he'd had a car waiting for us outside of the train station.

It was packed in there. We walked through crowds of kisses shared among families and life long friends. My tentative disposition began to relax as we paced ourselves through the people

Outside was a black Rolls Royce Phantom, the Drophead Coupe, with the top back. A hefty man with a bronze frame, wearing black slacks and a light gray zip-up sweater, was leaning on the driver side door. When he saw Zig, he smiled, and greeted Na and me. "Hello, Madame." His "H" was silent. "It is always lovely to see you." Nani kissed her teeth and said, "if I were okay with you greeting me like you don't *know* me, I wouldn't be a person at *all*."

Nani gave the man a light push and threw her arms around his neck. They hugged awhile, then he took Nani's luggage and dropped it in the trunk, opened the door closest to us and ushered us in. I hadn't noticed I was smiling so much until Zig said aloud, "he already loves it here."

As we drove away, I was watching everything that passed. Abe, the driver, was a hefty man who drove with his left. We drove slowly as there were many people walking about the street. Watching me, Nani noticed that I had been enticed by some people gathering up the hill. She tapped Abe and pointed toward my gaze.

There aren't many cars on the narrow streets of Dozza so I felt humbled, and important. We drove right into a bush of people selling mints; garments; fabrics; pillows; hand crafted sculptures and oils; and all kinds of fresh fish, fruits and vegetables. There were people doing live paintings and a lot of singing. Zig said we would get out and meet Abe back in an hour's time.

There was so much to take in. Each person that we passed was smiling mildly and assertive in selling their product. I walked up to a wooden table topped with rings, necklaces, bracelets and earrings. I called Nani over because they were all so keenly crafted and beautiful, I knew she would love them.

I had figured her out very well in a short time. We had an instantaneous dependency for one another. I told Nani to pick a set and I would purchase it for her. She laughed, rubbed my head, and picked a copper bracelet with a rose quartz stone in the middle. The Italian woman who handmade the jewelry didn't speak much English but her energy was pleasant and patient. She smiled graciously and gave us kisses with the accessories. Zig stood back, watching us. When we returned to him, he said that he knew a café nearby where we could dine. "There is very excellent tea there. All kinds! Hibiscus... black... mint," he said while looking at Nani who replied, "oh, yes. I am dying for it. I'm not terribly hungry. I will full myself on sweet bread." "You mustn't be a native?" Zig asked. They laughed. They were a little bit sappy so I laughed too.

As we walked toward the café, I was noticing many flowers and how green the grass was. I hadn't noticed how brightly the sun was shining either. "How long will we stay here?" I asked. "I think I am in love." Nani usually likes to answer questions straightforwardly, but for some reason she neglected to this time. "Well... for as long as we'd like," she supposed. I hate vagueness, but I felt alright with it.

After about half a mile, we arrived at the cafe. The name was "Alfonz."

The inside was dimly lit, relying mostly on natural light. It was intimate with extraordinary interior design. The walls were lined with famous paintings and cushioned booths where couples sat close to each other, sharing space and pastries. Everyone was full of the company in front of them; there was no longing. There was a huge sense of contentedness in Dozza. I only realized it once I was back in America, desiring anything outside of it.

But anyway, we sat ourselves out on the patio. The three of us were quiet for a few, looking at the menus. "I am going up to chat with the baristas," Nani said and dismissed herself. Zig and me were left at the table. He folded his menu and sat it down. "Do you know what you're having already?" I responded to this gesture.

"Yes, it's called a zippuli. It is a dough, stuffed with potato and anchovy. I get two of them and I like to add egg with peppers." Nani returned with two bottles of Italian Merlot.

CHAPTER 4

SIGMUND

We finished half of the first bottle before our food even arrived and even let Black have a taste because it is not uncanny in Italy. At most tables, there were many bottles, unfinished pasta, and lip stained glasses. That is not uncanny anywhere I've been. As two waiters came out onto the patio with our meals, one realized me, as I am sort of a regular here. "Ah, how are you? Please, take. They did not tell me it was you. And your beautiful lady." Roberto took Nani's hand and kissed it lightly. "Please, it is always nice to meet you. Your boy, he is happy now I see. Please, let me get any something for you," Roberto said as he refilled our glasses. His black slacks rose above his ankles as he bowed and dismissed himself. Black looked silently; impressed.

Alfonz, the owner, met us at the door as we were leaving. We are good friends. I introduced him to Nani and Black, explaining that they needed to experience some culture because America was draining and that is why they are here. Black chimed in saying that it was his first time ever being away from New York City. Nani looked

at him and got a somber look on her face. Alfonz
saw the excitement in Black and said to him, "well,
if you made it here to Dozza, and it is beautiful, you
will see many more beauty in the world and its
people." This made Nani light again. Alfonz took
care of our bill and bagged the other bottle of wine
for us to take home.

Abe was waiting outside of the café for us, eating a
calzone. I opened the door for Nani and got into the
backseat with her. Black occupied the passenger
seat. He was rubbing the back of his hand against
the plush white leather and feeling the wood panel
with his finger tips. We were about ten minutes out
from my house. I've moved into a bigger space
since the last time Nani was here to visit. She left
me with much to think about. I looked down at my
watch to realize that we had been at Alfonz's place
for over three hours! I was so pleased with Na's
company, as I always am- and Black, his presence,
brought a different element to our lives. It was
interesting. I didn't know anything about him, but I
really didn't mind. He was pleasant.

   The top was still back in my Rolls Royce,
the weather still comfortable, sun still shining. Nani
and I were bubbly from the Merlot we drank. I was
turned toward her, enamored, smiling. I took her
face and kissed it. She laughed and kissed me more.

Black and Abe seemed to be getting along well. They didn't look back once.

"I have an evening planned for us tomorrow. You must be tired, so we'll relax for awhile tonight. We will get you and Black settled in. You'll love this place. It has a spare room for him too. Are you feeling okay? What's on your mind?" "You're so excited," Nani said jokingly to slow my interrogation. "But I really am. We have a guest, we're in a smaller town. I missed you," I smiled.

We arrived in front of my place. It reminded me of a lone Brooklyn brownstone the first time I saw it, but a little more modest. I put more personal thought into it and had it reconstructed to modernize it. The brick is a deep brown and, now, the concrete stairs leading to the door are rounded on the ends and the double doors are painted a navy blue with golden handles and locks. I had larger windows installed for meditation and sun gazing at its rise and set. I think that I also had Na in mind; she hates lights on in the day time. I have a gardner who tends very well to my lawn, making the shrubs change shape every season. "The place is stunning," Nani said without us having got inside yet. Abe parked the coupe, opened Nani's door and grabbed her luggage from the trunk, walking it up the steps and sitting it beside the navy door. Black bounced out of the front seat, leaving the passenger side door open and ran over to me. He stood with his back toward the navy door, more amazed by the landscaping and the view than the architecture of my home. This was sometimes my favorite part too. We were on top of a small hill, neighboring orange trees, very few houses, and a grape vineyard that belonged to Stefani Pouli, an Italian designer and good friend of mine. I've just now noticed that Black didn't have any luggage, so I sent Abe to gather him some comfortable clothes, toiletries, and sandals to hold him over for a few nights. I grabbed her luggage and Nani, Black, and I went inside. About fifty feet from the entrance of the front door, is the winding staircase that leads up to my master bed and bathroom. To the right of the stairs is the living room where I have an accented wall painted black. It reminds me of dominance. The furniture is a pristine white, to soften the place, with hints of turquoise and gray from the pillows. The carpet is white too, and next to the window there is a black, polished piano. There is original art all over. "Do you play?" Black asked, pointing with his thumb to the piano. I replied yes, and that I could show him sometime later in the day. I slipped off my shoes before maneuvering through the house and Nani and Black did the same when they saw me.

As I walked toward the stair case, I yelled out

to them, "get to know the place, I'll put these things upstairs. Abe should be back within the next hour with some clothes for you, Black. Just some casual stuff." We all went in opposite directions: Nani to the right, Black went left, and I was going up. I was feeling so full.

CHAPTER 5

NANITA

I sank my feet into the thick, white carpeting in the den. I was so impressed with how kept the place was. I understood that we removed our shoes to revel in the luxury. To God be the Glory. I studied some of the paintings up against the black wall, fingered some of the sculptures. A few of the paintings were the most famous photorealism works of Chuck Close, blown up to such the perfect size that you couldn't tell the difference between it and a digital portrait. On the other side of the house, Black screamed out "beauty!" I walked over to acknowledge his exclamation and was surprised by a hazel-eyed, snow white Pit Bull. Black was sitting in front of her with his legs crossed, rubbing her back excitedly while she kissed him with her pink, wet nose. I stood back watching and noticed her Gold collar so I asked Black what it said to figure her name. Before he could lift her collar to tell me, Zig had come downstairs and into the kitchen where we were. "Her name is Belle. She is the sweetest. I got her just last winter and she has grown so much already. How could you tell she was a girl?" he asked. "We have the same femininity and features," I assured him. We both laughed.

Belle was in the perfect environment. The marble floor she lay on looked so smooth against her coat… so preen, I imagined her to bark in the Queen's English. Belle's attention was called away from Black when she heard her name. She got up and pranced over to me and I knelt down to rub her. Her crisp coat was cut low and she smelled like lavender, not much higher than my shin. Belle sniffed me out as though to make sure I was fit enough to live here with her. I think that her nudging and licking my face was the green light for our stay.

I hadn't taken off my jacket yet and began to feel a little tired. I wrapped my light fur around a chair in the kitchen and sat down in it.

Zig was standing at the glass door of the patio where he had just let Belle out to roam the lawn that was freshly cut, about two days ago, and a healthy hue. Black, who followed her, was totally engaged by her majestic presence, like any man is with women who know their beauty and power. There were toys in the yard that he summoned Belle with and it reminded me of new love how excited they were to interact with one another.

Zig turned away from the door, toward me, and smiled. "What's to you?" he asked. "You always talked about a Rottweiler," I respond intuitively, my feet propped up on the chair next to me. "And you always wanted a Pit. I saw her and I could not resist. It may have been her eyes. They have no end. And she was so sweet and glowing. She's kept me a lot of company, being here alone so often. I'm so glad you've come." Zig walked over to me and took both my hands in his. "Come. Let's go up. I know that you must be tired," he said with his eyes. I stood up, he dropped my hands, and picked me up and ran with me; the balls of his bare feet braced us on the marble floor. I was laughing so hard in delight that I could not even walk once he let me down at the spiraling steps, so he picked me up once more; onto the stairs, up, and into the bedroom. At the double doors, I stared into a dream.

The room was its own palace. The customized bed was the size of two California kings by both dimensions. We could raise a family in it. But I had not even been in Dozza a full day with Zig and had already been forward thinking. The last time I was in Italy, I wasn't ready for the fullness of his love. I became pensive...

a little uneasy. Zig had walked up three small steps that were inside of the room and into the bathroom to shut off the low pressure water I heard running. I collected myself and followed him. A copper colored claw foot bathtub, big enough for the two of us, was filled with pink rose petals, hot water, and a soft jasmine scent. There were so many pretty smells in his home. The tub sat atop a sheep skin rug that stood out against the travertine flooring. "It's waiting for you. I'll go and check on Black. Relax a little. I'm going to sit you a towel right here. There is a pen and a moleskin journal by the bathtub. When I come back, tell me a short story." He left. I undressed and looked at myself in the decorative, full length mirror that matched the copper of the tub, then stepped into it. I submerged myself into the steaming water thinking about how Zig knows that bathing is one of my favorite things to do to relax. He was subtly bringing up all the things we'd learned about each other over the years. "This is a movie," I said aloud to myself. "This man is a movie!" I began writing...

"The thing I love most about hot water is that it is a kind of delicacy and it reddens brown skin too. I really don't know what I hoped to do, bringing a kid here, but I could see that he, like a lot of brown people, have not expanded their experiences. People like us—like Black, Abe, Zig and me—our experiences as people who look even remotely the same, are always immensely terrible or beautiful. Now, for those who are full enough on the smaller things, you can never tell. Because maybe they never watch foreign movies in a language they can't understand, so therefore they have no longing. For some odd enough reason, I am so peculiarly bothered by this. It is such a phenomenon to me that some people do not know that there are entire places out there, in the world, that are Heaven already. In part, though, it is because we have only ever been given a dividend of our freedom. Manipulated into nationalists, ironically, we won't leave America willingly either..."

I closed up the journal with the thought that I can always take myself into some kind of misery, then I remembered the wine we brought home from the café. *Perfetto.* I lay back in the tub, letting the jasmine lighten me, breathing steadily as the water covers and uncovers my breasts.

Sigmund wakes me by splashing water on my face. He is shaking his head, finding it funny that I could fall asleep in water. "We were born this way." I sit up and smile at him. "I love you," he says and lifts my leg up to wash my feet. "What is Black doing?" I had to ask. "Abe has brought some things back for him. I showed him where he would be sleeping and he is taking his time getting to know our place." I pondered why he said "our." Was it a slip of the tongue? Zig chuckled at my pensiveness. I always feel that he knows exactly what I am thinking. "Abe asked if Black gets bored, would we care to send him over to Abe's place, since the kids are around Black's age."

"Well, what did Blaqueran say?" I asked. "His eyes lit up," Zig hunched. "He asked if he could meet them tonight. I was sure you wouldn't oppose, but I offered him the suggestion of waiting until you came back downstairs before leaving."

BLAQUERAN

They are treating me so well and just like family, so I do not feel intrusive, but I was a little afraid of what I would be doing here, and how I would be able to fall all in if I never left their side. When Nani came downstairs I was sitting with Abe and he was telling me how he'd grown up in Lagos and moved his family to the states, and then Italy when his oldest son was still young, so his chickadees were practically Italian-African-American. Liza Jane was the one I wanted to know more of. I couldn't wait to meet them. "So should I bring anything with me?" I asked. "You don't have to. My wife, Moni, is probably preparing dinner now. I will just introduce you to dem. We will return later, now." I was more excited to meet some friends than I was to be traveling at that moment. You need people around that you can be loose with. People older than I am don't get dirty or loose in the same way I like to.

It was around six in the evening when Abe and I left for his house. We left the coupe in Zig's driveway and took Abe's Infiniti truck— he had a full family. The truck looked brand new, except for a dried up, unordinary, red mud on the tires. We drove for a bit before I asked Abe, "what do Liza Jane, Avant, and Molten like to do for fun?" "You will ask dem" was his response. I wanted to keep the conversation up so I went on saying "back in New York City, I was always doing stuff. It was the most fun when it was frightening." "How you know Nanita?" Abe asked. I thought for a little bit and said, "She's my God Mother." I meant that in every literal sense. I sat back in the passenger seat, pleased with my answer. We rode with *Teacher Don't Teach Me No Nonsense* by Fela Kuti playing softly.

Nani called Abe while we were driving. She was trying to talk through tears and the only thing I could make out was "don't bring him back." Abe put the phone on speaker and I could hear Belle barking in the background. She was the only one protesting my removal. I thought I could hear Zig laughing in the background too. I was looking at Abe, wide-eyed, and I couldn't help the tears that fell. He hung up and said that he didn't have room in his home to house a strange boy, so he would have to let me out here. He stopped the car on a dirt road and unlocked the doors. I had been so foolish not to expect this abandonment. I was only familiar with the backs of people in my country. I got out and dropped to my knees as Abe drove away. I looked behind me to a tree who had uprooted itself and was showing its fangs, coming right toward me...

When we arrived at Abraham's home, the slow, sticky ride through an auburn colored goo rocked the truck back and forth and woke me out of my sleep. I was relieved to realize I made it through the drive. It was a contemporary, very elegant home. Abe announced that it was made entirely of recycled shipping containers, stacked and bound together with traditional building materials, made just the way he, his wife, and the architect had envisioned. He had earthed up some soil from Africa and brought it to Italy to build his home, here, atop it. A light rain had made it wet, and that is how it dried on the rims of his truck.

Moni, Abe's wife, stood at the door with her arms akimbo, halfway smiling. Liza Jane rushed out of the house and into her father's arms, sending a wind past me that carried her scent. "Eh eh," Moni responded to her daughter's excitement. "Come now, Mo. Your dad is home, Avey." The boys appeared at the door and kneeled to greet their father. "How are you, Sa. Is there anything to get from the vehicle?" one of the boys asked. I assumed he was the eldest. "We have brought it now. Black, this is my family. My wife; my three children- Molten, Avant, and my fine gal Liza," he introduced them with his hand extended toward each of them as he said their names. "He has come for Zig and Nani. He only has the dog to play with there so I brought him to meet you guys." Liza hugged me and Mrs. Odu asked Abe and me in the same breath how Nani was, and if she's planning to settle herself down and stay this time. I looked up to Abe who was laughing and he said "maybe, maybe not."

We all walked into their home together. The inside was colorful and it smelled like spices. From their ceiling, there was a globe hanging down like a chandelier. "I want to finish cooking," Mrs. Odu said and dismissed herself, Abe following. The other three kids ran off in their own direction and I was left standing there. I looked up and around, studying the place. This was the second most beautiful home I'd seen today.

Just the *smell* of Mrs. Odu's cooking made you full. Avant ran toward me and grabbed my shoulder and we took off into his room where Molten and Liza were building a fortress out of pillows and blankets. Avant sat me down on top of one of the pillows and threw a bed sheet at me. "Make something with us. You shy?" he asked me abruptly. "Man, that's not even in my vocabulary. I just don't know if y'all are cool or not yet," I shot back with a grin. I got up and popped the bed sheet open like something hot out of the dryer and it fell over Liza's head, covering her. We all laughed. I tied a corner of the sheet to the railing of the wooden bunk bed. We made a pyramid of blankets. Once the makeshift fortress was standing, we brought in small speakers and Molten's MacBook Air to play music from. Liza brought books, more pillows, and a desk lamp from her own room. Avant brought in a string of plastic doves for decoration. We settled in our place of secrecy and comfort.

"The food is ready oh!" We heard Mrs. Odu yell from the kitchen. We jumped up excitedly, being reminded of our hunger. We were busy sharing stories and laughing at each other. Abe had showered and changed into more comfortable and traditional clothes since I had last seen him and he was already seated at the dining table, his wife setting his plate with a mountain of what looked to me like grainy mashed potatoes topped with collard greens, in front of him. Mo, Avey, and Liza Jane waited in the kitchen with their plates in hand. "Go and bring your plate," Mrs. Odu directed me and pointed toward the cabinet on the far right above a stainless steel dishwasher. I pulled down a white, rectangular plate. Molten's plate was filled first. I whispered to Liza, "what is it?" "My favorite," she said and stepped up asking, "Can I have the snail, Mommy?" Avey let me go before him. Mrs. Odu took my plate. "Is this enough for you?" she asked. "It's plenty. May I ask what it is? I don't think I've had anything like it before." "This is Samol. It is a grain. And this is Efo. It's a spinach and fish and shrimp and meat dish. I put the red soup over it for more flavor. You will like it." "Thank you," I said and took my steaming plate to the table. I sat down to Abe's family, unfamiliar, but comfortable. They were all eating with their hands, grabbing the samol, along with the efo and soup, with all five finger tips. Abe had a fresh bowl of warm water he dipped his fingers in after every few mouthfuls. I mimicked them, thinking how exciting it was to be eating with our hands. The food was so good and rich. Avant, Molten, and Liza were all eating with their mouths open, making smacking noises while Abe was biting into the fat of a cubed piece of meat on a bone and sucking it out of his teeth, while Mrs. Odu was talking to him in Yoruba. This all felt so free.

CHAPTER 6

Sigmund had wanted alone time with Nani since her arrival. Now, there would be no one around to take her eyes when Zig would stare into them. Delighted, Zig had filled two glasses with the Merlot they brought from the restaurant while Nani was back upstairs detangling her black girl hair, long as it was, running coconut oil through each section that she parted. Zig put on a Billie Holiday vinyl, one of their favorite musicians; made a plate full of wheat crackers, strawberries, pineapple slices, and olives. He brought the hors d'oeuvres to the room with the piano in it. At the back of the room, there is a tall table with two chairs, and that is where he sat the plate and brought the wine.

Here comes Nanita, down the stairwell in her almond colored, satin robe. She goes into the kitchen and does not see Zig so she walks to the patio to watch the sun setting. Over the trees, the sky is a tint of purple, orange, and blue.

There is Belle, laying outside on her belly and looking with the same contentedness as Nani.

Her food and water bowls are still fairly full and, anyway, the patio door is always open for her to come in and out as she pleases. Nani whispers to herself, "thank you, God," and goes into the next room to Zig playing the piano along with the cadence of Billie's Blues. She sings along, "*I love my man. I'm a lie if I say I don't...*" Nani dances around, moving her full hips and shoulders; lifts herself up on her toes, spins, peels herself out of her robe. Zig is watching her; mellow, but his dick is erect and he is still pressing down on the keys. Nani dances harder, swinging her light brown hair... is naked now. The record plays the next song and Nanita pulls Zig into her body; puts her body on him. He cups her breasts and bites the right side of her neck. He uses his tongue like a paint brush, coloring her neck and ear as she responds with her strength- grabbing his waist, making him sway. Nani pulls Zig's shirt over his head, partially exposing him. She kisses his lips, his neck, his chest... bends her knees to lick his stomach. There is pressure in between her legs.

Nani slips Sigmund out of his slacks. His briefs leave next. She is at his feet, moving her hands up his thighs and he pulls her up into his arms, spins her, and leads her to the table of hors d'oeuvres and wine.

They sit down in one chair together, exposed, Nani on his lap. Zig moves the hair that falls down his girl's back to one side. They grab their glasses and toast to themselves, to their future, and the everlasting vulnerability they have with one another. *"Good morning, Heartache. Here we go again. Good morning, Heartache. You're the one who knew me when..."* says Billie. Zig bites into a strawberry. He is a very good man.

Nani wakes up around one o'clock in the morning with Zig laying next to her on the white carpeting. There is nothing left of the hors d'oeuvres but the leafy green tops from the strawberries; the wine, of course, not wasted, but finished. She kisses Sigmund with pressure to wake him and he does, smiling. "I could fuck you like this everyday," Zig says, and they go up the spiraling stairwell and into the room that shares the length of the entire downstairs.

Within the next few hours the sun's rising wakes them. It is around six now and a cool breeze is moving through a crack in the window, whisks the silk, rosé colored sheets that dress the bed, and snuggles Nani closer to Zig. Ruled by Venus, he had a love that was always welcoming. She told you he was magical.

BLAQUERAN

We ended up convincing Abe to let me stay the night and I slept on a pallet in Avant's room in some old basketball shorts he gave me. Abe came in to wake us with Liza Jane hanging on his back saying, "good morning oh. The phone is for you." "Hello?" I said. "Darling, we miss you. How was your night?" "Hi, Na. I'm just waking up. What time is it?" "Well, it's noon darlin'. You must've had an enjoyable stay." I paced around the house talking to her. "What did you guys do while I'm away? I know you must enjoy each other the most in your alone time. I'm having such a time here. It's different... fun," I said. "Sigmund is on the other side of the room figuring things out for Marrakech on Monday. We're just getting up too. I will ask Abraham to bring you over within the next few hours because we must be leaving here tomorrow by 4PM. Ciao!" I ended up in the kitchen by the time our call ended. I was looking out of the window at a Blood Orange tree and hadn't noticed that anyone was in there. "Black, you can't greet?" Mrs. Odu snapped at me. She was at the stove making eggs, tilapia fish fillets, and boiling sweet potatoes for breakfast. "I'm so sorry! I didn't realize you were in here," I said with a little embarrassment.

"Good morning, Mrs. Odu. How are you?" "I'm fine. I'm cooking. Tell everyone to come and bring their plate." "Okay... Did you guys plant that orange tree in the yard," I asked before leaving. She looked out at the tree too. "It just arrived there one day, as big and fruitful."

A few hours later when Black and Abe arrive back at Zig's house, Zig is playing in the yard with Belle and Nani is writing. This feels like a familiar scene for Black who gets out of the car smiling and greets them. Nani looks at him over her glasses which she is only wearing for decoration. She is...

I am all but lonely. I am filled by the pleasures of being in intimate company again. I am dealing well with company that keeps my mind off of television and news since, anyway, there is only one here and it hasn't been turned on once since we've arrived. There is just a bunch of feeling going on. Even I have to keep my mind off of the history text books sometimes and look to faces that are fresh and familiar; that rise my emotions like the increasing sound of horns in jazz songs. I lay my body down and allow love to lift me. I am floating again and it is just pleasant to love a black man who is strong willed and feminine; filled with melanin that turns him golden; meticulous; adventurous; seductive; and potent. It is pleasant to love a black man who is a painting, and a mirror, and a lion; gallant! His love, and God's, puts me in good spirits. It has always been an interest of mine, as a writer, to remain mobile and delicate. While I have been many places, there was never a plan for me to see the whole world- it is my personal longing that has always taken me there. It used to seem unusual that a black girl would travel away from America while everyone else is dying to get there. It used to seem usual that there was no other place for us in the world if we were not even wholly accepted in a country we have bled for. Sure, America, in its many theories, is the home of the free and brave, but it has always stifled us. It has, mostly, made us forsake our mental... the intellectual capacity that proves: whatsoever we think, shall be. We have not been abled in a way that speaks to us specifically, and so, I have taken a boy who has never been whispered to, and am trying to put him on a mountain top. This way he can see the world is finite, but no longer make himself, or blackness- in its divine order- apart of this such finite and casual existence. He will learn how to really be free.

Blaqueran and Sigmund switched positions- Black to play with Belle and Zig to speak with Abraham. Nanita stepped inside to check her email that is linked to her cellphone and saw a missed call from her friend Blye back in the states. Nani remembered their last conversation and the uncertainty she felt in her body about not knowing where she truly comes from and trying to figure out where it is she wants to end up. She decided to call him back, in all innocence.

Before he could say anything besides "hello?" Nani was burying Blye in declarative sentences- "I don't need to *know* to feel... You challenge me, but have only made me feel as extraordinary as I already know I am. You have never brought me beyond myself, though you've tried. You're calling just a few days after we've seen each other when you usually don't turn up for weeks. What else?" she ended her rant to ask. "I know we didn't mean to get so involved with each other and even though I never felt like you were in love with me, I got you pregnant to see what you would do, and only then I would have assured myself that the distance between us is healthy. When you text me to say that you..." -he stumbled- "...terminated the pregnancy, I felt foolish, but relieved that I wouldn't be tormenting myself anymore. I always knew that I was never yours." Blye paused and asked, "How is he?" He sounded so melancholy. Nani sighed and said, "I am here in Dozza with him. I was beginning to die trying to fight myself and my desire for this fulfillment. He is the only man that has treated me Whole without him and allowed my autonomy until I, naturally, ran out of my sole intention for independence. He's never made me feel like I need him, and that is what I've been attracted to for so long. We'll be off to Morocco in a few mornings, but I'm glad you called. I am trying to remember you for what you were worth, and let you go at the same time. Please, allow me." This conversation with Blye brought Nani back down to Earth and put even more certainty in her desire for Zig.

God is always relevant in my movement. Since waking up without a sense of self in New York, meeting Black, and bringing him to Italy where I have someone who feels like home, I know that God is always relevant in my movement.

Nani returned to the yard feeling lighter. Sigmund arranged the transportation to Marrakech with Abraham while Blaqueran begged Nani to stay another night with Abe's family. She was reluctant to impose on the Odu family, but Abe allowing, and reminding her that he would be back in the morning with Blaqueran in tow to take the three of them to the airport, Nani agreed. This worked out perfectly for the evening Sigmund had planned for the two of them. His good friend, Stefani Pouli, who lives just over a hill in an elaborate mansion something like Gatsby's, was having a cocktail party that Zig and a plethora of other artists had been invited to.

After packing an outfit and toothbrush for the night in a vintage, Ralph Lauren, vachetta leather duffle Zig had never used and so passed on to Black, he said good bye to Belle, kissed Nani on both cheeks the way he saw people at the airport in Venice do, and hugged Zig. Abe and Black were off, and Nani and Zig were to themselves again.

Nani watched Sigmund against the sun as he walked toward her smiling. He truly was as dark as a shadow, and so, so sweet. Nani turns her eyes into cages, hoping he will forever be lost in them, as she is lost in him.

SIGMUND

Once Abraham and Blaqueran are away in the distance, I lean over to Nanita and kiss her neck. I noticed she was writing while sitting here on the steps earlier. "Read me something," I say to Nani. She smiles and recites something from memory.

I have always fallen in love again in the middle
of it-
Sometimes atop your shoulders
The day begging at your feet
Letting the breeze of your breath consume me
I've wanted to worship something instead
so I took myself to the moon and the seasons
Trying to love someone as fully as I read a book
or, as holy as I think of wine
Hello,
Do you remember me?

"I love the way your words make your living. Many people don't use language the way you do." Na smiled and stood up to go inside. "I'm going to make a call, Darling. I haven't even mentioned my whereabouts to any *other* one I love." I followed Nani inside but headed to the kitchen where Belle stood beside my feet, gave her some water and drank some myself.

Since I feel like being smothering, I started up the stairs where Nani is. I heard her say into the phone, "Bitch, I'm in Italy getting back rubs in a French bathtub." She cackled laughing as I walked in and I knew by the way she was laughing who she was talking to. I was smiling too and said, "send Jordan my regards. How is she?" "Oh, here he is now, J. He says 'hello.' I'll talk to you soon," Nani says before hanging up. "You are just like the parrot of a pirate," she teases and jumps on me. I instinctively catch her and lay her at the edge of the bed and I can hear her thinking, "he is watching me as if he is filming me," as she laughs nervously. I go to the other side of the room where the closet is to show Na something inside. "Come here," I say to her. "For what?" "This is a Stefani Pouli dress I had made to fit you," I say as Nani rises off the bed to see the dress closely. She gasps. It is a black and olive green, floor-length tulle gown with hand embroidered sequins that will intricately reveal particular parts of her curves. "It is such a unique design! You know him?" She is holding the dress up against herself, strutting, while squinting her eyes and pursing her lips. I am watching her as if I am filming her. "Stefani lives right across the way. He has just begun a new business venture and has invited us to come and celebrate. Will you wear it tonight?" "I have the perfect shoes," she responds, and then, "what time will we be going?" "His invitation is for seven this evening" I say, and Nani's focus turns to the wall with a large, 3D fashion clock as its decor. "Well, it is just about four. I'll make us something light to eat before I start to get ready. Will you draw my bath, Baby?" "You don't run nobody," I say playfully as she heads down to the kitchen. I hang the dress in its place in the closet. I'm used to it being quiet, but since she's come I only want to fill the house with moans and music, so I run her bath water and put *Baduizm* on shuffle. It's still one of our favorite albums. I dim the lighting to draw more attention to the sun before it is overturned by the chief of the night, light an Egyptian Musk incense, and by the time *Drama* is done playing, the bathtub is properly filled, and I hear Nani call out to me. I head down the stairs into her beckon as the song changes to *On and On*. Nani is snapping to the beat, I grab her by the waist, and we Step.

Chicago shit. "What'd you make?" "Kale and salmon salad with some tomatoes, red onions, almonds, caramelized pecans, banana peppers and sautéed bell peppers. It should hold us over until the party." She kisses me and we sit at the kitchen table to eat.

"I didn't know you knew Stefani Pouli. He's well known in the states. I did a write up on him for a Vogue issue. He has some incredible pieces." "The dress upstairs, I helped him design it- though he didn't need me to. Yeah, his work is very spectacular. We met one afternoon driving to Alfonz. My car was a bit behind his the whole time there so I thought he must live nearby me. Once inside, Alfonz introduced us and I learned about his designs. He invited me over for a drink after our lunch and we have gotten to know each other very well." "What of Morocco? I haven't been there before. You are full of making my dreams come true." "I have two shows, one Tuesday evening and another on Wednesday. I thought we could stay until Friday and just enjoy the people for the rest of our time. I went a couple of months back just for the experience and met these guys who are fans of my music, own a concert hall, the works." "Everything is always aligned for you, Black Man. You just can't hide your magic," Nani says with a comforting seriousness. I examine her visually, and my smile is keeping the main attractions of Stefani's home a secret.

We head upstairs after washing our salads down with room temperature water. "I made the bath hot so it would still be okay once we finished eating." "Thoughtful you," Nani says and unbuttons me. We undress and watch our naked selves in the lengthy mirror, our skin glowing against the sunlight and copper things. *Baduizm* is still spinning. Once submerged in the water, we relax on opposite ends, our legs fitting between each other's. Finally, "What do you think of Blaqueran?" she asks me. I am quiet awhile…

"The youth is a light and fragile package, I can tell. I don't know much of where he comes from, neither does he probably. The depths of such information is not easily obtained. He's East Coast as shit though, which is cool, but with it being so busy in those streets…" (I am loving how, unconsciously, her lips separate themselves and her mouth sits slightly open while she listens.) "… People don't find much time to look into themselves and put their substance at the forefront. I think that being young and black is his gift. I think that he will use it, as we have." "I agree," Nani says.

"I am just trying to find a way to cultivate the enthusiasm he has. So much goes on in the world around us. I want to separate Black from formality and introduce him to dynamic. Truthfully, I bet he never imagined that people who look like him live so well." I chuckle at how fragile she is making him, and how his existence translates to people of color almost as a whole. "People have truly made it seem like a rarity. I can name five of my good friends, and ten of theirs, who have enriched their experience as black men and women just by developing the confidence to do so. Representation matters. Plus, we are not a people prone to stiffness." I end the conversation by lifting her leg to kiss the bottom of her toes. I pull her closer by her ankle, up her shin, and, lightly, by her thigh. I was in the mood for her moans.

Nanita lay back on the bed, breathless… the sweat on her upper lip drying. Sigmund turns on the fan to cool them. "I know you ain't tired," he says. "We have about an hour until Stefani will be expecting us. I can't wait to introduce you two. He's your style." "Can I catch my breath?" Nani is sure to ask before she rises from her relaxed state. She is completely satisfied- a feeling she hadn't felt in quite some time before the day she met Blaqueran. His youthfulness, paired with her own, aligned them. Zig begins to rub himself down with a jojoba and tea tree oil mixture; Nani notices and smiles. "I put you on," she says, referring to her introducing Zig to the Almighty powers pure jojoba oil possesses. He holds out the jar of oil to her and Nani follows suit, moistening every part of her body with its nutrients, paying special attention to her breasts, her bottom, and the heels of her feet. She hadn't even noticed the full bottles of some of her favorite fragrances sitting on top of the dresser next to Zig's own collection. There was Gucci's *Rush*, *Chance* by Chanel, Marc Jacobs' *Daisy,* and an oud by Bond No. 9. She gasped, and went straight for *Rush*- a "*shishk*" by her inner thigh, just below her breasts, and once more on her left wrist. Her mother used to tell her that the good shit didn't need to be so heavily applied. Nani rubbed her wrists together and blotted the backs of her ears so that her

Gucci fragrance would have the affect of a whisper when she acquainted people tonight. She went for her makeup bag and toward the bathroom -after putting on her lace, black panties- for just a bit of mascara on her top and bottom lashes, and bronzer to highlight her bone structure. Her eyebrows' thickness make them sit low and closer to her eyes, which compliments her naturally dewy look. Na runs her fingertips across her eyebrows to messy them for exaggeration. Her skin is glowing and something suggests she add a dark red to her plump, downward facing lips- the lipstick enhances her cupid's bow. "Perfect," Zig says aloud while looking at her from across the room. He is halfway ready, dressed in a creme, deep v-cut blouse and an all black, velvet-lined tuxedo jacket, fit to his very length and width.

    The Pouli dress being backless is a sexual elegance, and the copper bracelet with the rose quartz stone added a perfect softness to Nanita's look. Her heels are architectural- high as a skyscraper- and puts her right underneath Sigmund's nose. "You look beautiful," says Zig. "We compliment each other very well," Nani replies. "How are we getting there?" "I've called us a Black Car. It'll take us right to his door. The driver is waiting outside when you're ready, Mama." "Should we be bringing Stefani anything?" Nani asks as they head down the staircase. "Of course! This is why I have you, to remind me of these things. There's some Perignon we'll take. Tonight will be such a frolic." Once they reach the bottom stair, Zig takes off toward the back of the house for the champagne and Nani grabs her fur stole wrap, tucks her clutch underneath her arm, meets Zig at the door and they head into a dazzling night.

When Nanita and Sigmund arrive at Stefani Pouli's abode, there are limousines and two seater Porches parked, and people entering. "Let's wait for a bit," Nani says, and, both, Sigmund and the driver are patient. The three of them are watching people dance up to the door, women turning up their flasks and tucking them away before entering. "It looks like a lot of fun," the driver adds. "Is it true what they say about his home having spirits?" Nani looks at Zig with wonder. "I've never encountered any. We'll be going now. I can get the door," Zig responds while opening it. Nani steps out into his hand and the two of them proceed up the many steps to the circular door.

It is already open and there are two men dressed in tailored suits standing to greet them. "Sigmund Aku! How nice it is to see you. Your darling lady?" one of them says. "Nanita," says Zig. "My forever love." Nani blushes as the man takes her hand and kisses her cheeks. Another guy, smoking a cigar and holding up his glass of brown liquor on the rocks sees them by the door and immediately ends his conversation with the other party goers to greet Na and Zig. "Sigmuuuund," he sings in a rich, Italian accent. "What have you brought me? Who is this marvel?" he asks referring to Nani. "Nanita, meet Stefani Pouli."

"I see you are wearing my design. It fits you peeerfectly." (He is still singing.) Nani throws her head back dramatically, her hand up, and spins. The three of them laugh with their mouths wide. "Zig! I can tell we all will get along well." All of Stefani's words fit together perfectly with so much emphasis in the middle of them. Sigmund hands him the bottle of champagne. "Oh, you dare bring me more treats? We have plenty to drink, dear. But, oh, it is Perignon! Let us save it for the three of us," Stefani says and hands it off to one of the men greeting people at the door. Before they were off, "The men of the house, Meo and Betto," Stefani said and gestured toward each of them. "Come, come. Meet the band," Stefani excites as Zig and Nani follow him through the house into a room of people where four men were playing.

The lead singer was caramel complexioned, and she glowed like her trumpet. She was her own Louis Armstrong.

Get God on the phone

I can't talk no more

My baby gone and walked right out the door

Done broke my heart in two

Get God on the phone 'fore the fire's gone

He has the month of May in his skin

Might in his esophagus

He taunts my sanity with orange lashes he paints my

physicality amber when I have long believed in

cinnamon

She was singing in such a cadence throughout the room that Nanita was fixed on her… her long slip dress… the deep cleavage and high slit in it. Nani focused on her legs being long… brown… thick. Nani felt fingertips on her lower back that jolted her attraction. The singer had been looking straight into her face until Nani turned away to meet Zig's eyes. Another man appears holding a platter of cocktails and flutes. Both Nanita and Sigmund take up their preference of drink; Nani a sweet rosé, Zig a whiskey- straight. Stefani's attention had been grabbed by a group of four people; one with "locs" down to his elbow. "Would you like to…"

Nani was interrupted when another called out to Sigmund, stepped straight to him and grabbed his face. Sigmund held up his drink so as not to spill it. He reluctantly engaged with the French man who pinched his cheeks, but his eyes were darting back and forth in search of his lover, just to be sure she was okay. But she is always okay.

Nani danced around the room, Sigmund kept up with the people, and Xalla scatted while Nanita sipped an almaretto sour. Zig was making his rounds around the room, his eyes getting brighter with every upturn of his glass. When the ice would clink, Nani would look over to him, wink, and carry on. Many of the women were dying to know who she had come with, whose design she was wearing, and if she was from the east or west of the states.

Nanita was stunning. They were calling her "Beauty." Her aura was so casual and elusive it made the band players' tempo steady rise, getting more upbeat to keep up with her wit. The way she was moving through the crowds so comfortably was enticing. She invited people to the floor to dance with her, her tongue getting looser with every upturn of her glass.

Xalla and the band were on a fast number and she was singing with her neck, hands, and heart- bellowing from her belly. "Raise y'all's glasses right now," Xalla said. The people that made up Stefani's home tonight cheered. Xalla, too, commanded the crowd. "To our fulfillment... Must we never have to compromise what we desire in love." And they all met glasses. "We tired now, my band and me. You won't mind if we step into the crowd for a few? We'll spin a record for you in the meantime, how that sound?" They whistled and yelled *"viene con me!"* *"Buono"* *"Ti amo!"* *"Dai!"* and blew kisses.

Xalla pulled out a vintage cigarette wallet with a crown embroidered. She pulled herself away from the compliments and kisses and headed out back through a gazebo door. Nanita followed her into a vineyard and rose garden. They were both astonished by the unexpected beauty and should have known as much for a castle-like home.

"This place feels like the roaring '20s, innit?" Xalla said once she noticed Nani. There was a twist in her dialect that would not reveal her. "Where are you from?" Nani asked.

"Oh, every where, Darling. I've got family out in New York..."

"Some as far as San Francisco. I grew up in the south of France, played in Greece for years, stayed in NOLA for quite some time for my studies. I'm a musician, Baby. Home is where the melodies is." She handed Nani her lit cigarette. "I have been in Dozza just the last few weeks. Et tu? You are for Sigmund, yes?" She redirected the conversation for clarification. "I'm, foremost, for myself," Nani assured. "Sigmund and I have known each other since nineteen. You know him well?" "Not well enough for it to mean anything. Stefani met us all together just last week. I know that he sings himself. Beautiful boy though, yes?"

Nani took a drag of their cigarette and stepped back some, sizing Xalla. The songstress laughed, stuck out her long, polished leg, and lit another cigarette. Just then, more people joined them in the garden.

Everything, for me, seems more fluid in Italy. I've always loved its rhythm.

"You speak with a very familiar rhythm," Xalla said to Nani. "*Faire l'amour ici,*" she teased in her French tongue while walking away. The vibration between them was fervent.

In the garden where Xalla left her, Zig startled Nani with a whisper in her ear. "Bring her home," he said. Nani was longing, and he hated to deny her anything. Besides, the woman was interesting enough to tolerate, beautiful enough for their common desire, and all out phenomenal in her craft which, mostly, was to woo. "I'm having a marvelous time, Ziggy. I love you," Nani replied, flicking the cigarette butt, swinging her arms around Zig. He puckered his whiskey drenched lips and she entangled him with her slick tongue- kissed his face, his neck, his soul.

A love like this is rare. Love that is as fluent as language and so free. This was a love that exceeds insecurity and limitation. They practiced for this sort. It had not always been this way, especially in their younger days being more sculpted by traditional expectation. Since tradition is made up of geographical customs and beliefs adopted by generations, the thing that has exposed them to this "full of life" feeling is travel. With every where they have gone, tradition differs. The people in new places reach for what they want and do not hold it too tightly and do not know constraint. This kind of free had to be learned. And it is easier this way. New territory summoned this lady and her man, who had *been* together in many ways, to cool off... to have more *true* experiences together. She hated entitlement and he hated indifference. Somehow, peninsulas became their respite. Traveling exposed their truth. They became more able to communicate their desires in foreign lands. He would never deny her. And so, "bring her home" Nani would.

For what it's worth, Xalla had been well aware of the plot since they walked in. You could practically smell their essence. Since she had met him prior to this vernissage for Stefani's gallery opening, Xalla knew Zig to be a charming man with snow white teeth, signaling a healthy appetite. He had an equally masculine and feminine appeal that helped Xalla to translate whom, or what, he was. And his lady matched him well. This songstress wasn't needy in love. She, too, liked to feel free and pleasured. "What a treat," she was thinking when Nani met the room.

Zig and Nani were encompassed in a slow dance to the faint sound of Ahmad Jamal at the Blackhawk, when Stefani approached them, drunk and smitten. "I did figure to find you two here in my garden," he said. "It is the most beautiful of all my place. You will have to come in light to see the grapes up close, Nani." "Maybe tomorrow for an early picnic," she suggested. "Beautiful, I hope we will recuperate well enough," Stefani said and held up his glass. Then, a man walked by and tugged Stefani's ear, redirecting his attention. The man had olive skin, long black hair slicked back into a low ponytail, and a full beard. He nodded toward Sigmund, acknowledging him, and waited for Stefani to properly introduce him. Stefani addressed the man in another tongue. What he said in Arabic, which Nani understood, translated to "my sweet boy." "Nani," Stefani said with emphasis on the "E" sound at the end of her name, "Sigmund…. meet Alvah." Alvah hugged them, and Nani spoke with him in the thick, richness of Arabic. It was the most she had gotten to know of anyone the whole night. Alvah could have a pleasant conversation with Nani without making her existence solely about her appearance. He didn't make Nanita an enigma. She found out the reason for the party was because Stefani had just rehabilitated his late father's factory and would be premiering it as his art gallery tomorrow. "Join us in the morning," Zig said turning the conversation over to English. "We'll come over for brunch in the vineyard."

"We'd love to have you. Is that going to work okay, Stef? We all know of the busy day tomorrow."

"Yes, of course. I have a heavy size family. I am used to budgeting my time wisely," Stefani was saying with a smile.

"Na and I have a late flight to Marrakech. I'm playing there and I think we'll stay awhile."

"Oh, Marrakech is beautiful, beautiful! Good luck, you two."

"Inshallah. Let's get back to the party," Nani suggested and led the way.

She picked up another rosé and made her way over to Xalla, who was mingling with the band. Zig was in tow.

One of the band players noticed them walking up and gravitated toward Zig, having the pleasure of meeting him and expressing his admiration. They call him "Zo" and he has great expertise in percussion, is why he respects the combination of black man and piano. Zig was flattered. Nani politely interrupted to bring Zig's attention back to her. She was saucy."Hello, Sigmund," Xalla said and stepped toward him. "How are you, my darling?" he asked and kissed her cheek. "Your voice is beautiful, Lady." "Thank you," she blushed. Just then the music got loud and "C'est Chic" got everyone to revel in the night and their drunkenness. "Come, let's dance!" Xalla grabbed both Sigmund and Nanita's hand. Was she making the first move?

Anyway, the band was dancing and the ladies were swaying, making their bodies into symbols. No one was afraid to get too close to someone else. They jumped up and down to the rhythm, spilling champagne; Nani and Xalla both well into their several flutes of rosé and shots of whisky. Xalla was up against Nani- Zig was fanning them, encouraging the sensuality between the girls, obviously enjoying the moment and heat they were creating in the room. They knew not sophrosyne, but all of indulgence and reciprocity.

"How you so selfless?" Xalla shouted to Nani over the music. "You and your man, you have too much fun together."

"Well, isn't it better this way? Some people let love ruin them... ruin their autonomy. But there are so many ways to be in it."

"In love?" Xalla asked to clarify.

"In lust; in like; in curiosity. It's better to be receptive of these behaviors. At least the ones that are not so destructive."

Their faces were close now. Zig was grooving with the rest of the party, Chicago-style stepping and snapping on beat. He was moving. Everyone was feeling the rhythm of Sigmund and Nani's kind of free and it was making Xalla intensely attracted to the both of them. When Nani and Zig are together, they are so beyond worry. Each other's presence promotes the comfortability one has with a best friend. They shared everything. Even through the times they were with other people, Nani and Zig stayed available for one another. Xalla wondered where she would fit in, but didn't let the thought consume her. She wasn't going to be intrusive. "Show me," she told Nani and kissed her neck. "Have more fun than feelings," Nani said and took Xalla's hand, leading her off the dance floor to a seat. Xalla was ready to fall all in.

Sigmund danced away from the women that were on his heels and made his way over to Nani. Xalla was there too, sitting pretty, but his eyes just were not made for her. Pleasing Nani was his only pleasure.

"Ziggy, I want to show Xalla the palace. I think we are ready," Nanita said, looking over to Xalla. "You girls go ahead. I'll meet you there within the hour. Let me call your car now," Zig responded. Xalla suggested that he shouldn't worry. She would have the band's driver to take them. "It's just over the hill, innit?" she asked. Zig smiled at her. "It is," he said assuredly with a nod. He kissed Nani and spun her around. "There are too many who love you," he said. "Ciao, bella." "See you soon, Ziggy."

Xalla went to let Allen, the band's driver, know where she was headed. "I can show you the way. It's just a short distance. You can see our place from the garden," Nani assured Allen. Xalla laughed, mentioning that Allen was on pay roll and didn't need an explanation. "Come, now."

Nani kissed goodbye the people at the party, saved a date to see the band play again, and blew warm kisses at Sigmund. Allen opened the door to the SUV for the two boss bitches and they climbed into the backseat. Once they were settled in the center of the backseat, Allen drove out of Stefani's driveway and onto the narrow road. Xalla was sitting close to Nani, looking at her through the rearview mirror, watching her lips as she mouthed the turns to Allen. Xalla became entranced. She lay her head down on Nani's lap and kissed her pussy lips through her gown. Allen was concentrated on the twists in the road. Nanita was tingling. "And just up this hill, Al," Nani said as they met the palace. She lifted her lady's head. "We've made it."

Belle was waiting in the window and greeted the ladies at the door. Nani kicked off her shoes and Xalla followed suit. They headed up the spiraling staircase, barefoot and filled with booze. Just as they reached the top of the stairs, Xalla stopped Nani and kissed her with a wide mouth. She kissed each lip separately; she kissed her cheek; she kissed her neck and unzipped Nani's dress. She kissed her shoulder and let the gown fall, spilling onto the floor. Nanita was so allowing. She felt Xalla's pearl through the slit in her dress. The V-cut in her gown was inviting and encouraged Nani's attraction. Xalla took Nani's hand from underneath and stuffed it into her cleavage. Nani grabbed Xalla's breast like she owned it. This sent Xalla to Nanita's feet. She squeezed her thighs and kissed her pussy through her panties. She kissed around her waist line and pulled Nani's panties down. She was left barely able to stand as Xalla pressed her mouth into Nani and used her tongue as a muscle. She grabbed Nani's bare ass cheeks and spread them, almost entirely lifting Nani up onto her face.

Nani was on her toes and gushing, rhythmically moving back and forth to the song on Xalla's tongue; ad-libbing with "yes" and seductive moans. When Nanita opened her eyes, Zig was watching from the bottom of the stairs. Already barefoot, he took off the jacket to his tux and folded it across the banister. Zig's eyes were swollen with desire. He headed up toward the girls, Xalla still at Nani's feet. Lightly, Sigmund grabbed Xalla's hair and ran his fingers through it. He joined her at Nani's toes and they kissed each other. Sigmund lifted Xalla out of her dress and led the girls to the room.

CHAPTER 7

When she woke up, Xalla was in bed alone. She sat up and studied the room. From a bit of a distance, she heard water running, and got up toward the bathroom. From inside of the claw foot bathtub, Nani was leaned over, writing... the water slowly rising.

"With the elaborateness of love, it is not difficult to understand the longing of nowness and an abandoned love thought conquered. Sometimes I'll miss you. It is the fight of past and future. It is the overcoming that can ruin love or watch it stay. It is not difficult to understand and imagine the fullness of what an all inclusive love with different men and women would feel like. Love is big enough, isn't it? Monogamy has constructed what seems like discipline, but what is actually the weight of wine tasting, matinees, as many children, opposing ideas, passion, and affections put onto one person.

People are more complex and needy than one relationship might handle. The demand of handing over all desire to one person at a time is a conflict we try our best to live with. But in actuality, it limits our capacity for love. It limits life. It limits, in many ways, experience. While many relationships outside of the home may be strictly platonic, there is often a sense of distrust among lovers within the household. We allow our human fallacies- of insecurity, of jealousy, of leverage- to deny us the fullness of the human experience. The Western world has separated everything into two- the sun and the moon, the right from the left, the man and the woman, the earth and the heavens- as opposed to the harmony of one all, all one. They only want to count to two. But what will we gain by sailing to the moon, if we are not even able to cross the abyss that separates us from ourselves? I am very much out of touch with the totalitarian idea of love. Please, allow me."

Xalla stood by the door, still naked, watching Nani write. She hadn't yet noticed Xalla standing there. "'Ello. May I join you," Xalla said in a raspy voice, sounding more French than before. Nanita looked up and smiled, put down her pen and sank herself in the water. Xalla stepped into the tub too. It is just 8 AM.

The girls were sitting across from each other in the tub, laughing, when they heard Sigmund coming up the stairs, talking loudly on the phone. He walked into the bathroom and waved to acknowledge them, wet his toothbrush and continued to shout. Sigmund looked at himself in the mirror as he talked business between brushing. He spit, and rinsed. "Alright then. So we're out at five? Sounds good. Ciao." He turned around to face the girls. "Good morning, beauties." "Morning, Ziggy," Nani replied. "Good morning, Mr. Magic. Will you bring me a smoke?" Xalla asked to see how much of an impression she had made. Sigmund returned to the bathroom with the rolled up tobacco, handed it off to Xalla and struck a match to light it for her. She leaned in to the fire in his hand, trusting him enough to look into his eyes while he lit her cigarette.

Xalla tightened her jaws as she inhaled the smoke. Satisfied, she leaned back in the clawfoot bathtub and thanked Zig. Nani stood up and stepped out of the tub, her feet warmed by the heated tile, and rinsed herself under the shower head on the far side of the bathroom. Xalla and Zig were talking lowly. Xalla asked, "how is it that this feels so pure?" to which Sigmund responded with a chuckle that meant, "just let it." He undressed himself as he walked toward Nani. Before reaching her, Zig turned back to Xalla. "You eat a lot of cranberries? Your pussy is very sweet tasting." Unorthodoxly, Xalla took a drag of her cigarette and smiled. "Honey, I juice. Cranberries, oranges, apples, and ginger. A real recipe for my girl things. I mix up bananas, pineapples, flax seed, leafy greens, and maca too." Zig winked at her with "noted" in his smile and joined Nani in the shower. He grabbed her wet hair from behind, put his body on hers, and nuzzled her neck. Xalla stood up out of the water and said to them, "your kind of love belongs in a novel." This enhanced their passion.

Xalla watched as the heated tile quickly dried the excess water that rolled from underneath the glass door of the shower. The room got steamy. She opened the drain of the tub and showed herself out, thinking "they have evolved my melody."

To be continued...

CPSIA information can be obtained
at www.ICGtesting.com
Printed in the USA
FSOW03n1848061217
41972FS